Wealth Lost, By Yours Truly,
Divorce

Wealth Lost
By Yours Truly,
Divorce

D. LAMONICA

Wealth Lost, By Yours Truly, Divorce
Copyright © 2018 by The Kang, LLC.

Cover illustration and design by Rebeca Covers
Book design and production by BB eBooks
Editing by Dominion Editorial
Printed by Kindle Direct Publishing

ISBN-13: 978-1-7325810-3-6

All rights reserved. No part of this book may be reproduced or transmitted in any form or by any means without written permission from the author.

This is a work of fiction. Names, characters, businesses, places, events, locales, and incidents are either the products of the author's imagination or used in a fictitious manner. Any resemblance to actual persons living or dead, or actual events is purely coincidental.

"They say war is hell. Divorce is hell."
DIVORCE

Chapter 1

Introduction

HELLO, EVERYONE. SORRY to sound so arrogant, but I'm so into myself. I am a legend and a curse to some or to the millions that know me. Every person that is single or married thinks about me. That's why I'm so powerful. I am in your mind before you even think about doing the deed. If men or women aren't thinking about me, I'm at least in the back of their minds. You can't help but think about me. It's you who keep me alive and around for so long. I thank you for that.

My name is synonymous with the Grim Reaper himself. I am a reaper in my own right. I constantly make you think, what if I had done this? Could it be saved? What could I have done differently to save it? I am feared, dreaded, and loathed by thousands upon thousands of individuals. I cause pain and sorrow due to missed opportunities for reconciliation. I am a powerful force nearing god-like status. I should be a god. Many of you damn near worship me multiple times without even knowing it. I watch successful families crumble before my very eyes without shedding a tear. Remorse is a feeling I've never experienced and know nothing about. That's your job. That's your emotion.

Once you say my name, I cannot have remorse for you. If I did, I wouldn't be who I am. My favorite supporters are attorneys, mediators, and judges and sometimes the sheriff and police. They don't come cheap. They work in unison to bleed you dry of every dollar you have to come kneel before me at the end of your fairy tale. And you *will* kneel before me. You will kneel at my feet. It is inevitable.

Let's face it; I'm a rock star. I generate so much money from your pockets for my supporters that it should be illegal. My supporters bask in your failures in life. Not one of them cares about you. Their only job is to serve me in the end, not you. I am their god. They serve me. They get paid, and all you get is a handshake and maybe a pat on the back on the way out the door as they tally all the money you've poured into their pockets.

My power increases when the thought of me burns in a married man or woman's brain. As I said before, you create me without even knowing it. Once I am a fixture in your mind, I will never go away. You and I are bonded as one for life. My powers burn so steadily in a married person's brain sometimes, that they are even willing to commit a crime, just to get to me. Men and women throw all their good character out the window and actually commit a crime to lay a hand on me. I've had more hands laid on me than the Pope himself. However or whichever way you choose to run into my arms, it doesn't matter to me. As long as you call or reach out to me, I will always be accepting to you no matter if it's legal or illegal. No one will know.

My supporters couldn't care less as well whether it's the truth or lies – as long as they're getting paid. Eventually, you will get to me, and all that criminal activity will be forgotten and swept under the rug just to end your union. I will not comfort you though. Comfort is for the weak. I am all about getting to your happy ending. You would like to think it is a happy ending, but it never is. Scars for life remain after you deal with me. Many will fall on your way to see me. People you love will suffer because of you. These things I leave in your hands to deal with because I care nothing about them. You can find comfort someplace else because I am not the one for comfort. I hope you do find comfort in a second try at marriage though. Because I will be waiting again for you to call my name with open arms. I will come running to you, always during that time of need. We will always have a special bond you and I after the first marriage.

My aura is so great around me that 40 to 50 percent of married couples in the United States will experience me first hand. So, when you are in front of the pastor on your happy day, and he is saying all those words out of that little black book in his hands, many things are going through your mind. I'm one of those things. It's impossible not to think about me. When you get married, you should find you a good attorney and place him on retainer for the future. The odds that you and I will be meeting one day favors me. You think your god and the little man that sits at his right hand can save you from me. I have looked God in his face and spat at his feet. This union of marriage is mine to control, not his. This god of yours may lay down and make the rules, but rules are made to be broken. That's when I come in. Even your god can't stand up against me. I break his rules and laws on a whim if I want to, and he does nothing. Pray to him all you want. He can't save your marriage from me. Once my foot is in your door, you might as well give me the key because I'm here to stay.

I don't care about the mental, physical, educational and social problems your offspring have because of you trying to seek me out. That's your problem to deal with. Your first marriage will more than likely see me 41 percent of the time. You must be a pure optimist going into marriage. Before you even say I do, you've already been predestined to fail. That's just the way it is.

I don't want anyone to be lonely though. That is not my intention. I can't survive without the institution of marriage. It's what keeps me going. Without marriage, I wouldn't exist or become more powerful than I already am. My favorites are the ones who marry multiple times. My hats off to them for giving marriage another try. That's what I like about men and women. Everybody wants someone to be with, no matter what. You are programmed that way, and because of that, I will always be around. Everyone wants and needs that special someone near them. So, I encourage you to give it a second try. I will be there with you each step of the way almost 60 percent of the time. That second time you try at marriage, more than half the time will end in failure. I'm glad you don't research these things – which makes you oblivious that you're walking into failure once again.

And even after that second unsuccessful try at marriage, I'm not a fair-weather friend. I will be with you until the end no matter if it is a sunny day or a hurricane, I will be there for you. I say, give it another try. Third times a charm is what I'm told. This most definitely is the one. At least, in your mind, you think it is. On this third try, I will be with you 73 percent of the time. What that percentage says to me is as soon as you get married, you may want to go ahead and find a good attorney to have on standby. Because it's already written that your marriage will end in failure sooner rather than later. Go ahead and place that attorney on retainer after the honeymoon is over. Every time you get married, I get stronger and stronger each time. The bond between you and I can never be broken after the first marriage. Always remember that. We are friends till the end you and I.

I am a patient friend. I usually wait eight years before I solidify our friendship. Once I have ended your first marriage; I wait patiently again for you. That is how much I am committed to this friendship of ours. You will never have another friend like me, and I only do this for you because we are the best of friends. I usually wait an average of three years for you to get married again for the second time. As I said before, I'm a patient friend. When you do make that move for the second time, it brings so much life back into my spirit. I am filled with joy for you. It shows me that you truly do care about me and this friendship of ours. Unfortunately, I can't reciprocate that feeling, but I will make it up to you when you are single again. I promise.

My favorite age is thirty years old. Such a tender age thirty is. You would think at that age, you would get smarter, but unfortunately, you don't when it comes to marriage. But like I keep telling you, I'm always there for you no matter what. I'm so there for you that I will wait another three years for you to get married for the third time. That's three times I've waited for you. There should be no question how loyal I am to you at this point. Not even your own god pays attention to you as much as I do.

When you do get married for the third time, I am so happy for you. Even on your honeymoon, I am with you as you lay in bed after a night of hot, steamy sex thinking about a prenuptial agreement. I laugh at prenuptial agreements. It's too late now. I love the thought behind prenuptial agreements. I'm there when you sign the papers. I have my hands on both of your shoulders at that meeting. It's like you've already planned for me to be in your life forever. It brings tears to my eyes thinking that you cared about me so much that you would plan ahead for the demise of your marriage. You're the best friend ever. I knew you cared about me just as I cared about your marriage. That's why we will always be together whether you're single or married.

This work that I do requires minions that go about to do my bidding throughout the course of each marriage. They are, for the most part, a loyal following of my most trusted companions. Every now and then, we don't see eye to eye on certain things. But in the end, if the path towards me has been set up by them correctly for your marriage, I don't have a problem with these companions of mine. My favorite companions in life are named Marriage, Infidelity, Temptation, Finances, Communication, Arguing, Weight Gain, Unrealistic Expectations, Lack of Intimacy, and Lack of Equality. There are a whole host of other friends I hang out with, but these friends are my favorites. I like them like candy; maybe even ice cream.

How rude of me. I ramble on and on about myself, and I never introduced who I am. I am the end of the road for all marriages. I am the reaper and the breaking of the bond that you had created under your god. The bond that your god created between you and your spouse during your marriage can only be broken by me. Just think about it for a second. Not even your god can or will break your bond of marriage. That's my job. That's why I'm here. Only through me can you seek salvation from your spouse once you have deemed that you don't want to be married to that person anymore. The only way to break the bond that was created through the power of God himself is through me.

Lucifer has nothing on me. My realm is between heaven and hell. Whether they like it or not, I'm a god in my own right. Many seek me out without even knowing it. Your thoughts are what deceive you and what give you away all the time. Your spouse can't see them, but I do. Because I'm always there. Those thoughts are what lead you into my warm embrace. There are only a chosen few who can resist my power and use this special word in their marriage to defeat me. I will never speak its name. That four-letter word diminishes my strength every time it is spoken. I hate it!

Those chosen few who can actually speak the four-letter word and have the faith and heart behind it are a dying breed. Long gone are the days of forever being married like your parents or grandparents. I threw everything I could at those people. My companions and I gave it our all in hopes one of them would follow the path towards me in saying my name. You have to say my name for me to take over. It is required for me to come to life. But people like your parents and grandparents are special and have a special kind of bond that not even I can break. That four-letter word within them was real. I watched as my companions would bring an onslaught against your parents and grandparents and they still wouldn't break. For that, even I must show them my respect. Not even a god like myself could split them apart.

Long live this new generation. They keep my powers growing and keep me and my supporters ever so busy. I am more than separation. Separation is for wimps. When drastic measures are required to end a marriage that is when I am at my strongest. When my name is spoken out of the mouth of a husband or wife, I love the way there is silence between them when they are face to face. That silence is so serene. It is a quiet that calms me while I watch as the bond that was created by your God crumbles right before your eyes. It is one of the greatest sights to watch. A holy bond between two people coming down like the walls of Jericho. Only a god can do that.

I probe into the mind of the husband and wife when my name is spoken and watch visions of happier days racing through their brains. It's almost like watching your life flash before your eyes before you die. This is death in a way. The death of your marriage at my hands. I am the reaper of marriages that have gone to the wayside. These visions of the wedding, the honeymoon, the first house, the first child, the family time together, family vacations, and many more visions of happiness that race through each of the minds of the husband and wife are meant to break you down. Those visions of happier times make your knees buckle, and you eventually will be at my feet kneeling, crying, saying my name. Once you say my name, your path is already set. It's a journey thousands have taken before you to seek me out. DIVORCE is my name. I am the end of your fairy tale story of marriage and the beginning of a possible nightmare for you. My happy ending is the demise of your marriage. Once I get steam behind me, there is no stopping me. I laugh at your god. He is powerless to help you. Call his name. I dare you. I am your master and lord now! I am the force that is sweeping this country and the world. Believe me when

I say, there isn't a god damn thing you can do about it once you are in my clutches. Once you say my name, it's a done deal. I come like a freight train at you. I'm a juggernaut. Once I start, I can't be stopped. Your four-letter word and your god can't help you now. You belong to me once you say my name.

One of my best friends in the world hates me. It hurts sometimes, but I get over it. You ask, how can two best friends hate each other? I get asked that question all the time. There is a simple answer to that question. One can't live without the other existing. Once there is a union between two people and my friend Marriage has come into existence, I then can come into existence – me, DIVORCE. Without my friend Marriage, there can be no me. Marriage always comes first. I wouldn't mind being first, but it doesn't work that way. I've learned to live with that though. Unfortunately, for a lot of married couples, they usually do not live with the thought of marriage being first in their lives and in their minds. Because of that, I will come in second, and I don't mind playing second string. Because when I take to the ring against my dear friend Marriage, our friendship goes out the window for that stretch in time. With my companions in my corner, Marriage doesn't stand a chance against me. That four-letter word and your god are not enough to save you from me and my companions. Your marriage is weak. Your defenses have holes. My war against your marriage never ends. Eventually, I will weaken Marriage.

Marriage is a delicate thing. I constantly chip away

at all of Marriage's defenses against me. I throw so many blows at Marriage only the strong are willing and able to defend against my assault. I am not forgiving in the ring of life. My goal is to win always. I will make you say my name to weaken and break the bond of Marriage. Once that bond and wall around you have been broken, Marriage ceases to exist anymore. Only I exist now with you until the end.

And from your previous reading above, over fifty percent of the time, I will always win and be victorious over Marriage. One must die so the other can live. That's the bond Marriage and I have. We are in this constant war for survival. Long ago, Marriage had the upper hand. Now, it's my time to shine. Marriage has grown weak over time while I have grown stronger. Where is your god now, Marriage? He can't help you. Where is your friend? The four-letter word. It can't help you either.

No matter what you do. The only thing that can defeat me is a bond I've only witnessed and seen during your grandparents' marriage way back in the day. Now that was solid. Those were tough times for me. Even in their separation, they seem to always come back together no matter what. I was damn near powerless during those times. Marriage always defeated me back then. No matter what I threw at your parents or grandparents' marriage, they always seemed to survive through it all and defeat me. Marriage today has changed. It has changed in my favor.

I am smitten with Lust. Lust is a trusted companion of mine. Lust can make a man or a woman do anything thinking that it is that four-letter word. Lust has replaced that four-letter word in today's marriages which is to my advantage. Without that four-letter word in my friend Marriage's corner, it's doomed against me. I started winning fight after fight after fight. It's almost boring now knowing you're always going to win. Now, Marriage barely has a chance against me in the ring when we meet. My corner is loaded with nothing but the best of life's trials and tribulations to weaken the bond of Marriage during the fight.

I am, and I will win the fight. Marriage is weak now. The knockout blow is for you to speak my name into existence. When you say, 'I WANT A DI-VORCE.' I may be on my last leg. I may be down and out on a nine count. But once you have spoken my name, a new surge of energy brings me back to life. I stand back up on my two feet to face the bond of Marriage. I see your god in your corner shouting to you instructions on how to defeat me. But it was you who spoke my name first and turned your back on your god. You empowered me. You have helped me throw my winning punch to shatter your bond of Marriage to your spouse. Unfortunately for my friend Marriage, it's always a knockout punch that ends the union finally on my way to victory. I watch my friend Marriage laying on the bed of life as the bond is finally broken and it falls at my feet. I look down at my friend as it continues to struggle to stay alive and relevant. Marriage reaches out to me to try and help it up. But I turn my back on it. I can't cry for my friend Marriage as I watch its demise. I have done it for ions. I look over at your god and smile. I'm but a few who could actually look God in the face and spit on his creation. That's what happens when you give man free will, God. Man and woman will speak my name before they will seek you out. The fight between Marriage and I is to the death. I stand over Marriage and watch as it dies a slow death. I smile. I'm so used to winning now, I hardly even try anymore at defeating Marriage. I think the next time I step into the ring with Marriage, I'm going to tie one of my hands behind my back just to give Marriage a chance. I bet I still win because it's just so easy to say my name DIVORCE rather than fight to save my friend Marriage from the unavoidable beat down I always give it. You are already in my corner, and you don't even know it yet. You turned your back on Marriage, on your God and decided to come into my corner with me against Marriage, your God, and that four-letter word. But always remember, with me, you are always in the winning corner. Unfortunately for you though, the winning prize at the end is not happiness. Wealth will be lost at the end of this fight. You think it's all about money, but wealth encompasses many other aspects of life you never think about until you and I watch Marriage lay on the ground dying from the beatdown you and I gave it. You are the one who said my name and joined me. Your emotions and mental state mean nothing to me. Once that knockout blow is thrown, the ten count to get to the end of your Marriage is seconds away. You will always remember, it was done by yours truly, DIVORCE.

Chapter 2
Marriage Number 1

As I mentioned before, I have other friends and companions who assist me with the task of directing your marriage down the path where at the end, you will say my name. You can say these friends of mine are like signalman; they navigate you down the runway to your final destination which is me – DIVORCE. It is a complex roadmap to get to me, but once my friends keep directing you down the right path, it's quite easy to find me. If you are still confused, I will show you how you can find me. We will use a true life example. This young man is one of my favorite kinds of people who make the right choices in life when it comes to me. When I saw this young man, there was so much potential for him to meet me, and this young man even knew it in the back of his mind before he tied the knot. So, let's begin our journey with this young man as he makes his way not only through life, but specifically headed to a meeting with me he already knew would happen.

This young man, we will call him Anthony. Anthony is a twenty-year-old sailor in the US Navy. He's single and enjoying life until one day he meets an older woman named Janet in a nightclub one night. Situations like this bring new life to me. I love it when older women latch their talons onto a younger man. Unions like these always play into my favor most of the time. Old wants young; young want old. No matter the circumstances, the union between young and old usually leads to me. This young man doesn't know what the future holds with this older woman. I mean, he's twenty years old, and she's thirty-two years old with two kids. I love when young guys don't use the brain with the matter and use the brain with all the blood inside. When they use that brain with all the blood inside, it gets hard and makes bad decisions. Once it takes a plunge into that sweet nectar, even more bad decisions are made. This young man's thought process is not used to planning for the future at all. It's for the now. I mean, a thirty-two-year-old woman? He didn't even ask her if she wanted to have more kids in the future since she already had two. This is the kind of union that caters to me to the fullest. I already saw where this was headed before this relationship even happened. Unfortunately for the people that decide to marry, they don't think like I think – which is to my advantage and to Marriage's downfall and defeat. Couples don't think about and ask questions like, can I see myself with this person five, ten, or even twenty years from now? If you can't honestly answer that question and continue on with plans to get married, I'm all in with you. A year later, Anthony and the older woman he met in the club,

Janet, are married. When they were married, it breathed new life into me. When Marriage, the crowning jewel and favorite of God is created, I'm born as well. I guess you can call it the fight between good and evil. God never realized that I would become so powerful as to overshadow and defeat his favorite, Marriage. As I said before, I am like God almighty himself. My reach may not be as great as his, but I am everywhere. With each new marriage created in his name, a new replica of me appears for that new marriage. I am weak at the onset, but as time goes on, I grow stronger with each passing moment. Marriage and I are like the little angel and devil on each side of your shoulders. But when it comes to me, there is only one option to choose from, and it's always my way. Because in the end, you will say my name.

While out on a six-month deployment, Anthony meets my best friend. It's one of the leading causes of why people are directed to say my name. I love temptation. Temptation makes my mouth water for more. It makes my victim's heart beat rapidly. They start to perspire at the thought of meeting my friend Infidelity. Infidelity smells so good. Infidelity can be anything you want it to be. She or he is so beautiful in your eyes that you're willing to break one of God's laws itself to be with it. Because our subject is a man, Infidelity is a woman. Infidelity changes sexes to meet the need of my victims. I admire Infidelity. Our friend Anthony hasn't been in this situation before. Let's read his mind. I see Anthony going to church as a young boy. I see Anthony standing up and reciting The Ten Commandment verse, 'Thou shalt not commit adultery.' What a joke.

Just because you know and can repeat God's law forwards and backwards can't save you from my companion Infidelity's subtle attack on your conscious. You are weak. Just as I thought and knew all along. Anthony, just like everyone else I meet, knows right from wrong. That's why I love the fact that God gave each individual free will to do as they choose in hopes his people will follow his lead. I laugh at that concept all the time. You may not believe in religion but, you must admit, if The Ten Commandments are followed, you can live a good wholesome life. But knowing The Ten Commandments and following them are two different things.

That's why I enjoy how God gave man free will to do as he pleases. Anthony has a choice to make. This is a decision that will affect him for the rest of his life. He can choose to walk away knowing he has done the right thing during his separation from his wife while on deployment or he can make the decision to lay down with my friend Infidelity. If Infidelity wasn't my friend, I would call her a whore for sleeping with a married man. But I don't judge. That's God's job, not mine. I just wait to see how this all plays out.

Temptation is too much for Anthony. Temptation is sweet. He cannot resist the urges of the beautiful siren that is before him. I try to read his mind, but there is only sexual desire in his mind that has transferred down to the appendage on his body that is my favorite living being. Because when that appendage penetrates Infidelity; the path that he unknowingly has paved for himself to a meeting with me has already been set. Temptation has a hold on Anthony. He moves in. Just a few more inches. He's in there! The passion of Temptation through Infidelity feeds power to me. I begin to grow stronger in Anthony's mind. He knows he's doing wrong. That's why I'm on his mind. Thank you, Anthony, for that rush of energy has brought me closer to being a thought in your head once the deed is done. Anthony has allowed Infidelity along with Temptation to control his actions. Infidelity felt so good, but now, the conscious starts to play with Anthony's emotions. Leaving the scene of the crime that was committed against his wife, Anthony's thoughts dwell on what he just did. In one instance, I spring to life as a thought in his mind. I plant myself back in Anthony's brain. As he thinks about me, I constantly let him know I'm there for him whenever he's ready to move forward. Like I said before, in the beginning, I am immortal. I cannot die. Only one thing can put me down, but I'm never out. Anthony has allowed me to become a thought in his mind, thus a part of his life. I'm fully reborn now. I'm apart of Anthony now until the end. To fully realize my potential, Anthony must say my name to bring me forth.

I once heard the saying, 'Temptation is a mother fucker.' Anthony now must live with the thought of Infidelity on his mind. Along with Temptation,

Infidelity feels so good when it happens. But when it's finished, Infidelity causes the good within Anthony to conflict with himself. He knows what he did was wrong. I see in his mind that he keeps saying to himself, 'I have committed adultery.' Like I said previously, everyone knows right from wrong. It's up to the person to make the choice to do what's right and not what's wrong. In Anthony's case, he decided to break one of God's commandments. So much for repeating The Ten Commandments in church. It doesn't mean a thing to me. That commandment is garbage to me. Anthony hopes to keep what he has done hidden, but Infidelity doesn't like to be so easily swept away like she's nothing. Once you lay with Infidelity, you're connected with her for life.

Somehow, Janet got wind of his escapade while on deployment. She sent Anthony a letter stating what she had heard. I love rumors. Once the rumor reaches the individual, the story is so convoluted with bullshit it almost seems that it's impossible to be true. I have people beyond my supporters working for me. They are supposed to be friends and acquaintances of yours, but they will not hesitate to throw the husband or wife under the bus to ruin their marriage. Such is the case we have here. The rumor was that Anthony was living with someone overseas when it was just a one night stand. I just felt another surge after I read the letter Janet wrote Anthony. My sibling has been reborn, this time in Janet's mind. They both haven't been married a year yet and are already thinking about divorce. Couples like this are number one with me in my book. Their path is already set with a meeting with me. All any one of them must do is to say my name.

CHAPTER 3

Marriage Number 1 — Communication and Money

THIS NEXT FRIEND of mine is sort of an asshole. He's never just one way. One minute he's my friend and the next minute he's against me. I want him to be one way, but sometimes he goes both ways which is never good for me. When a married couple doesn't utilize my friend, he vanishes. I like it when that happens. The less I see of him, the more the married couple will continue to head my way. Communication is his name, and if it's always one way, then that usually means the highway for the other member of the marriage. It's when Communication allows two-way conversation between a couple that it makes me angry and forces me to show emotion. That pisses me off because there may be a chance that a couple on the point of saying my name may speak sense to one another and possibly do something I hate married couples to do. I don't even like speaking the word because I hate this word with a passion. The word is 'reconcile.'

My existence is always threatened if that clown Communication allows the married couple to speak carrying on a two-way conversation. If they are not yelling and angry with each other, a civil conversation could spell doom for me. You can say it's sort of a love-hate relationship between Communication and me.

What I want and need is what Anthony and Janet are currently doing in my favor. Janet is not writing letters while Anthony is out to sea on deployment. The only time he writes Janet is to ask for money. He doesn't even say he misses her – which tells Janet his mind is occupied with something or someone else wherever he may be. So to Janet, this rumor she heard may have some truth to it. This time, good ole Communication came through for me. With no communication going on during this marriage while separated, my candlelight continues to burn bright and grows stronger each passing day.

At the end of the deployment, when Anthony's ship pulls in, he and Janet hug and kiss one another like nothing ever happened. Communication has screwed me over again. Things that happened overseas have been forgiven, and I'm left powerless again but, there's still a glimmer of hope that I will strengthen again. It's only a matter of time.

Another friend of mine that helps to speed your marriage to an untimely demise is my associate Finances. When it comes to Finances, Communication should always be somewhere around but usually doesn't show up until things are totally ruined. Better yet, if Communication is around when Anthony and Janet communicate about Finances, they do nothing but argue with each other. That's when my fair weather friend Communication is on point and on the job for my cause. Finances and Communication go hand in hand when it comes to marriage. When there is no communication, that's when tempers flare and arguments happen. This married couple never sat down and discussed who would be in charge of the finances and what goals they had for the future. I love this couple. If there is no communication at the beginning about managing the finances, confrontations and arguments are going to happen. It's a given. As these confrontations and arguments keep escalating, that's how I keep growing stronger and stronger.

Anthony and Janet arrive at their apartment. Anthony walks in and sees that the apartment is completely furnished. Anthony asked Janet how did she get all this furniture? Janet said she used his credit to get the furniture. Since they weren't communicating while Anthony was on deployment, wifey went out and bought things to make her feel better with her good old Power of Attorney he gave her before he went on deployment. I love Powers of Attorney. Especially when wives misuse them for things they shouldn't.

So, now we begin to see what this older woman Anthony has married is all about – herself. Anthony was always a money saver, and this set him off. This furniture bill set him back with the high interest rate charged for the furniture. You think Janet discussed this financial decision with Anthony? Hell no. Janet felt she could do whatever she wanted. Now Anthony was stuck having to pay for this furniture through allotment.

I just felt a jolt of energy surge through my body again. I just heard the word 'bitch' said in Anthony's mind. Wow! This is great progress.

This relationship started off in a nightclub without really any kind of morals behind it which is a good thing for me. I can take you back to the very day Anthony and Janet were married. I was there when these two tied the knot. I was there at City Hall minutes before they were called in to be married by the justice of the peace. I witnessed as Anthony got up, but Janet, the soon to be wife, remained seated.

Anthony said, "Come on, let's go."

Janet just shook her head no.

You would think that Anthony would sit down and talk with his soon to be bride to find out what the problem was. But no, this pissed Anthony off. He paid damn good money to get married and he for damn sure was going to get married today. I like Anthony's thought process here. He could have sat down with his soon to be bride, found out that she didn't want to get married and be out about $100 in processing fees because she got cold feet. No harm no foul and that would have been the end of me. Instead, Anthony puts his foot down. I like it when a man takes charge.

"Get your ass over here so we can do this," Anthony said.

Janet got up and went into the room with Anthony. They got married. Talk about getting married under duress. I enjoyed the ceremony though. Quick and simple. Quite forgettable. Unfortunately for Anthony, it's not so quick and simple when it comes to me. He could have been out one hundred dollars, but instead, he chose to get married. When he finally sees me, he's going to wish he had just taken the signal from Janet, left the building and been out the one hundred dollars.

This couple continued to live their married life dancing and drinking their days and weekends away at nightclubs. When he took his bride home to meet mom, I was surprised to hear mom tell his son in secret, 'This is not going to last.' I'm with you, Mom. After placing that thought in Anthony's head, I became more of a fixture in his mind.

There was truly no commitment in this marriage whatsoever. Everything seemed to be going fine with this marriage, and then Infidelity pops up again. If you, as a married couple, make a friend out of my friend, Infidelity, the writing's already on the wall when it comes to your marriage, and that writing spells my name. Anthony went out on deployment again to come back to his car being repossessed due to the failure of his wife Janet to pay the bill on time. Anthony also found out that Janet herself had met my friend Infidelity. I guess what's good for the goose is good for the gander. Is there really a bird called a gander? I'll have to check on that. Where was I? Oh yeah… It was only a matter of time before Janet got her revenge on Anthony and now my friend Communication is back on the scene. This time I like what he's doing. There's nothing but constant arguing going on between this married couple who haven't realized the only thing they have in common is sex. Nothing more. I like that. It's always a recipe for disaster.

Chapter 4

Someone Will Speak My Name

AFTER A HARD day on the ship, Anthony came home and sat on the couch thinking while Janet was in the kitchen cooking. After three years of marriage, he had nothing to show for it but bad credit from his car being repossessed, a depleted bank account from the mismanagement of money by his older wife when he was out on deployment, and my best friend Infidelity wreaking havoc between the both of them. They couldn't talk without arguing and Anthony was tired of having a wife that just sat on her ass around the house all day only working when she wanted to. That's when I began to grow in size and stature in Anthony's head. I continued to unleash thoughts of a better life without Janet, to be single again, and to have more money in his pockets. I could finally hear the words in his head. Those words were sweetness to my ears.

'Get out while you can. Go back to the ship. Leave.' Anthony acted on those thoughts. He did exactly what I knew he would do. Anthony went upstairs while Janet was cooking, packed his sea bag with his uniforms, clothes and came back downstairs. I love this part. It just came out of nowhere, and it hit Janet by surprise as she was making dinner. I wish you could have seen the look on Janet's face when Anthony said, "Take me to the ship."

Janet looked at Anthony, and she knew he was serious. That's when thoughts began racing through both of their minds about the good times they both had prior to them getting married. Once those flashes were over, Janet didn't argue or say a word. She got the keys to the car and drove Anthony to the ship. They didn't speak a word the entire drive to the base. Anthony got out of the car and didn't say a word. He just began walking up the pier. He didn't even look back once.

Janet sat in the car watching Anthony walk away and said, "You'll be back."

Janet drove off.

A few days passed by with Anthony living on the ship. He hadn't seen or spoken with Janet since that night he left. Janet called the ship and complained that Anthony wasn't providing support for her. Once there is separation between a married couple, the supposed love that the two people had for each other dissolves and is replaced by self-preservation. Self-preservation – meaning that love is replaced with the need for money. Money is the only thing that remains in this marriage. There is no place for love between this married couple anymore, so money replaces that need just as it does in all marriages that crumble.

Anthony was counseled by his Chief onboard ship that he should seek out one of my biggest supporters –

an attorney. Anthony couldn't believe that he now had to find an attorney and speak my name into existence. It took him some time to say my name, but he eventually came around to saying it when he found a law firm to help him with his situation.

"I want to file for divorce."

There, Anthony finally said my name. It's hard to speak my name when you look at yourself as a failure. I am and will always be a failure in your life – if and when you say my name. Anthony failed at marriage just like so many other unsuspecting couples out there who think this is a joke. No, this is real life with real consequences for your actions. Anthony tells a fib to the lawyer that he and his wife have been separated for over a year to speed up the process. He wanted to get rid of her as fast as possible, and he figured Janet wanted the same. With a stroke of the pen and a five hundred and twenty-five dollar deposit, divorce proceedings were underway. I am in full effect now. Thank you, Anthony, for making me whole again. Thank you for saying my name. If this divorce remained uncontested, Anthony would get away with saving a lot of money in the end and for the future. But the damage and time lost has already been done. When you lose time in life, there is no way to get it back. Once it's gone, it's done.

On the drive back to the ship after meeting with my friend the attorney, Anthony thought about where his life was at after four years of an uneventful marriage with Janet. His first brand new car was repossessed ruining his credit – and his Aunt's credit who cosigned for him. He had no transportation. No money was saved or invested during this entire marriage. His savings account was depleted. There was no real property to divide because they lived in an apartment or government housing the entire marriage. Janet took the little furniture that they had acquired. After four years of marriage, these two had absolutely nothing to show for the time they were together. For Anthony, that was a good thing. At least he was still young and could start over. However, in the grand scheme of things, this was a wasted four years that could have been more productive and fruitful alone if Anthony had taken the advice of Janet that day down at City Hall. When Janet's actions in the courthouse showed she didn't want to get married, Anthony should have run for the hills.

My greatest enemy couldn't save this marriage because there was none of it in the beginning. I won't even speak my enemy's name because she is forever dying and withering away while I keep getting stronger because of young people like Anthony and Janet. That is four years Anthony will never see again. Wealth doesn't stop being lost when the divorce is final. No, it doesn't work that way. It continues to eat at your finances until the very last payment. We're talking years afterward. The marriage may be over, but the effects last for years afterward. Believe me when I say that.

The day finally came for Anthony and Janet to go before the judge for the final decree of divorce. The judge asked Janet if she wanted spousal support and she turned it down. The judge asked Janet again, and she said no again. Anthony was surprised. Even I couldn't believe that. A female turning down money during divorce? Wow! All Janet said she wanted was her last name changed back to her maiden name. That was it. Anthony got off easy with this one. The first in what I hoped would lead to a second marriage where Anthony and I could do business again.

When the judge hit the gavel, Anthony and Janet were divorced. My work was done here, but the effects of this divorce would last for years after the gavel came down for Anthony. It was Anthony who carried all the debt in the marriage. Janet had made sure everything was in Anthony's name. Janet got off clean with no debt in her name. She knew what she was doing when she attained credit in Anthony's name using the Power of Attorney. Now Anthony had the responsibility of paying off all the debt Janet loaded up on him during the marriage. Anthony was able to save a little money during the lead up to the divorce. He had enough money to place down on a new car. Outstanding! Good for Anthony. However, due to his credit rating being so bad, he bought a car at nineteen percent interest that wasn't even worth the amount he paid for it. But, Anthony was blinded by me, Divorce, so he went ahead and bought the car as a present for himself for being single now. Thank you, Anthony, for saying my name. Unfortunately for you, it will be years of wealth lost, by yours truly, DIVORCE.

Chapter 5

Marriage Number 2 – Infidelity and Finances

OVER FOUR YEARS have passed since Anthony divorced Janet. I'm but a distant memory in Anthony's mind now. That doesn't mean I'm gone. I lay dormant in the back of his mind as a remembrance of his failure at marriage. Anthony actually said that he was never going to get married again. I've had men and women say that all the time. There fooling themselves when they say they will never get married again. It's in everyone's nature to want to find that special someone to be with. Everyone wants to find that someone you can't live without. Fortunately for me, these men and women have short-term memories and continue to live in a fantasy world. They never sit down to evaluate what went wrong in the first marriage before jumping right into the second. It's because of that short-term memory that I stay relevant even if the person is not thinking about me. But trust me when I say, I'm always there for Anthony when he needs me.

This brings us back to our friend Anthony who is in a club again one night looking for a quick one night stand on a Sunday night. Anthony spots a target to go after. A lot of science goes into looking for the perfect one-night stand, and our friend Anthony is now a master. He is set to make his move, but low and behold, a beautiful Asian lady comes up to Anthony while he is sitting down slowly drinking on a beer he doesn't even like. The beer is just for show. It's a man thing. Anthony looks up and sees a beautiful Filipina standing in front of his table smiling. Reading Anthony's thoughts, for a Sunday night, he thought to himself he had hit the jackpot. To me, this beautiful Filipina I saw, was wife number two. The lady introduced herself and said her name was Nenita. She sat down with Anthony, and they began to talk. Anthony found out that Nenita was eleven years older than him. What's up with all these older women latching onto these younger guys? Eleven years older than Anthony, but you couldn't tell it by looking at her. She looked like a little China doll, and Anthony was all googly eyes for her. They talked for a long time about each other's previous marriage, what went wrong, and what they wanted to do for the future. I mean, these two are practically planning their future together right before my eyes. It was almost like two people being served to me on a platter. I liked this union.

Nenita was a single mom with an older daughter just starting high school. Anthony, of course, never questioned Nenita if she wanted any more children. He was still young, and children weren't even on his mind yet. She quickly allowed Anthony to move into her apartment with her and her daughter and took care of him like a king. Anthony had never experienced anything like the love and care Nenita showed him. Anthony moved into an apartment where Nenita treated him like he was already the man of the house. Blinded by the loving kindness of Nenita, Anthony fell right into her web without even thinking about it. I myself stay dormant while a man or a woman are engaged in this so-called fairy tale boyfriend-girlfriend relationship prior to the big day when they lock themselves into an agreement called marriage. I try to stay furthest from Anthony's thoughts so he can let Nenita charm him with her feminine wiles until the day of reckoning comes. I don't want him thinking about me when he should be focused on sealing the deal with this new lady he's found. Or should I say, new lady who found him? You'll see.

Nenita was going on one year of being divorced. She was depressed at how her marriage had ended. Nenita needed another military guy who could take care of her and her daughter. Hopefully, this next guy would be nicer than her previous husband. When she saw Anthony in the club that night, Nenita automatically knew he was the one that could fill the void as a provider for her and her daughter. When Nenita saw that Anthony had his sights set on another Filipina in the club dancing, Nenita knew she had to make her move before Anthony did. She got up and went over to his table and asked Anthony if she could have a seat. Anthony said yes. From that moment, a relationship blossomed. I was so excited for the both of them. I love when a new relationship is formed. From these relationships, comes marriage. And without my good friend Marriage around, there can be no divorce. And without divorce, there can be no me.

This relationship continued to blossom into something special, but Anthony was screwing up with his favorite pastime in my friend Infidelity. He wasn't even married yet. I can't have him screwing this up for me. I needed to manifest again, and I can't do that if this fool screws this relationship up due to his promiscuity. I needed him to stop cheating on Nenita for them to get married. During the boyfriend-girlfriend phase, everything must be in order for it to progress to the next stage. After the deal is sealed with marriage, Anthony can do as he chooses. One day, Anthony actually talked about having kids with Nenita. This could be a deal breaker for me. If Nenita can't have kids, then Anthony won't marry her. Nenita told Anthony she was unable to have any more kids because her tubes were tied, but that shouldn't stop him from marrying her if he loved her. She spoke that word I can't stand. I can feel it pierce through Anthony's head. He had to ask himself that question. Does he love Nenita enough to marry her? If you have to think if you love someone, then you don't love them. I can't believe I'm even speaking that word. Whatever the case was with Anthony, I needed him to marry Nenita. Love or no love, I am certain that he and I will be seeing each other again in the future. That word. I spoke it. Just saying it drains me. I must be more careful. I required

Anthony to act on his emotions rather than that four-letter word. If that four-letter word were involved, I would be no more. Nenita forgave Anthony for his idiocy and decided to continue the relationship with him. Once Infidelity has her claws in a man, the man or woman is constantly mystified by Infidelity's powers forever. That's just the way it goes. And for you men and women, if you have never heard these wise words before take heed – once a cheat, always a cheat. Infidelity is my favorite friend. Infidelity and I go hand in hand. Without that four-letter word in your relationship or marriage, one of you will be coming to see my friend Infidelity sooner than you think.

After about a year together of living as a couple, it was time for Anthony to transfer to shore duty. Anthony was unsure about what to do with Nenita. If Anthony was unsure now, then he was unsure about his feelings and his relationship with Nenita continuing at his next duty station. Anthony transferred and left Nenita behind. He said he would come back for her, but Anthony knew in his mind that it was over between Nenita and himself. This was bad news for me. However, Anthony's conscience started to get the better of him. I like that. There's that emotion causing him to think about Nenita. He knew in his mind he had found the perfect woman to be with in his life. Without question, Nenita was an awesome woman. Anthony's conscience finally got the better of him. He decided to bring Nenita up to where he was and marry her. He married her and didn't really love her. As we have seen in Anthony's previous marriage, that's a recipe for disaster to not really love someone you marry. When the 'I dos' were finished, and Anthony and Nenita were finally wed, I came back to life once again. I was present in Anthony's mind. He remembered me. I felt so special. However, he didn't remember the things that made his first marriage go south and now it looked as though he would repeat those same things again in this marriage. A guy like Anthony is a dream come true for me. With him by my side, I will never die. Anthony and other people like him are who made me damn near immortal now.

Anthony and Nenita were married and seemed happy together, but they were not. They were a great team working to save and invest money for a better future, but something was missing. Nenita saw Anthony as a cold person with no feelings toward her. There was hardly any communication between the two of them. Anthony let Nenita do whatever she chose to do just to keep her quiet and away from him. They had money in the bank, and Anthony didn't care what his wife did. Nenita began to substitute money for what she was missing in her life – love, that four-letter word again. It drains me every time I say it. Because she needed those four-letter words in her life that were missing substantially from her marriage, she spent money heavily to try and fulfill that need. Nenita did it right under Anthony's nose. Nenita was entranced with my dear friend Finances, who she totally ignored. Since there was no communication between Anthony and Nenita,

Finances, Communication and Nenita became best friends secretly draining any and all money from all Anthony's accounts. As long as Anthony had enough money to do what he needed to do, he didn't even pay attention to their joint bank account as it continued to dwindle. He also didn't pay attention to his credit card statements that continued to grow out of control due to his wife's misuse. Anthony didn't even know Nenita was hiding all the mail. Anthony entrusted Nenita with taking care of the finances. The same mistake he made when he married his first wife, Janet.

When Anthony's time was up on shore duty, he was transferred back to sea duty. Now that Anthony was back on sea duty, he decided to invest in some stocks for his eventual retirement from the military. He had planned on buying thousands of dollars' worth of stock from a company called Amazon. He needed to withdraw money to add to his brokerage account to accomplish this. When Anthony arrived at the ATM, he was greeted by my friend Finances. Anthony was unable to withdraw money. He knew he should have money in his personal account, so he drove back home to look online to check his balance. Once Anthony was online with his bank account, he found that his account was not only at zero but in the negative. The power of my friend Finances is unbelievable sometimes when it comes to money or lack of money. Now, my friend Communication steps in because there is going to be an argument. Anthony was screwed over at a younger age by Janet, and now he would have to go through the same thing with Nenita, the pretty little China doll who seemed like the perfect wife. From this moment, a can of worms was opened that began the downward spiral for this marriage. Communication can be my friend one day and my mortal enemy the next. Let's see how this goes.

Communication this day would have been my enemy if these two had talked about my friend Finances and vowed to work together like any good marriage to solve the problem both of them had now. But that, like I said, was for any good marriage. This marriage between Anthony and Nenita wasn't a good marriage at all and when I say that, rest assured, it's true. They could have possibly solved their problems if they had worked together as any married team should do. However, I'm not in the business of solving problems for my friend Marriage. Marriage needs to figure its own problems out and use its friends available to try and keep the marriage strong through this turbulent time. Get down on your knees and pray to your god above for help. I'm sure he's listening. Wait for him to respond. By the time he responds, you won't have a pot to piss in!

The secret finally revealed itself as Anthony discovered that Nenita had placed them in debt for over fifty thousand dollars. Wow! Fifty thousand dollars in debt. For a middle-class couple, that is a significant amount of money. With this discovery, Anthony recommended Nenita file for bankruptcy which continued the downward spiral of this marriage. Due to the mismanagement of finances by Nenita, this marriage continued heading down that yellow brick road. Anthony was at fault as well for not paying any attention to Nenita. There is no wizard waiting for you to fulfill your wish. I'm waiting at the end of that yellow brick road behind all the smoke and mirrors. This isn't the fantasy land of Oz either. This is real life. Anthony and Nenita fell to my two friends Finance and Communication after originally being a financially successful couple. Nenita told Anthony that she spent all the money because he never showed her any attention. Amazing! All of this could have been avoided if Anthony had shown his wife some attention. I guess spending all that hard-earned money got Anthony's attention really quick now. This couple never was the same after the bankruptcy hearing. They lived in the same house but lived separate lives. Anthony and Nenita went their separate ways while still being married. My friend Infidelity found itself into both the lives of Anthony and Nenita. Anthony came home from a short deployment to find out that Nenita had another man at their apartment while he was away. I could only laugh at this situation as I sat back and watched this convoluted mess of a marriage spiral its way towards the grave. That's all I had to do because eventually, someone will find the courage to seek out one of my favorite supporters in an attorney to say my name. That's all I'm waiting on. For one of them, to say my name. They were both committing adultery behind each other's backs now. Infidelity was catering to each of their needs. Anthony just wanted sex. Nenita wanted the warmth of a man next to her. If she couldn't get it from her husband, she would get it elsewhere. I'm relishing in the way this marriage is heading. Such a promising marriage at first. It's always like that; so promising in the beginning. Couples like this, solidify my place in the world as a god among men and women.

In Anthony's mind, I began to resonate more and more. There was nothing left in this marriage to salvage or to build on. Those stocks in Amazon he wanted to purchase were not even on his mind anymore. A major opportunity lost at the hands of his marriage to Nenita. Anthony wasn't getting any younger either. He sat down and thought about the years wasted with Janet and now Nenita. His second marriage was going down in flames. He kept trying to pinpoint on how such a promising marriage went wrong. His heart knew what went wrong, but he wouldn't admit to it. I knew what went wrong. No one ever goes into a marriage with the intent of seeing me one day. That four-letter word blinds the couple to my presence. But that four-letter word is the only thing that keeps two people from doing the things Anthony and Nenita have done to each other over the course of their marriage.

Anthony knew to progress on further in life, it was time to end his marriage with Nenita. Anthony dreamed of one day purchasing a home with Nenita once he returned to sea duty, but all those dreams had now been shattered. He wouldn't be able to purchase a house while married to Nenita. He felt in his heart this marriage needed to end. A big smile came on my face as

I sat back and watched Anthony plot the demise of his marriage.

The ship Anthony was stationed on was scheduled to get underway on deployment. Anthony moved Nenita from their large apartment to a smaller apartment. He placed all their extra furniture in storage. The story he told Nenita for the move was it was a way for them to save money when in fact, Anthony had saved up a considerable amount of money because he had cut Nenita off after she filed for bankruptcy. He didn't trust her with a dime of the money he earned. When the ship deployed, that would be the last time Anthony and Nenita would be together. He cut off all contact with her. When he returned, he found the same attorney who had completed his first divorce from Janet. I was waiting with anticipation for him to say my name once more. The paralegal asked Anthony the reason for his appointment.

Anthony said, "I'm here to file for divorce."

He said my name. Saying my name is like exhaling all your troubles away. Life was once again rushing through me. My friend Marriage was on the ropes again ready for a knockout blow from me. Once my name was spoken, all hope has been lost on reconciliation. When my name was spoken, I could feel Anthony's heart racing as he said my name for the second time in his life. But once he said my name and exhaled, it was complete. Saying my name is almost like opening the lock on a door and setting yourself free from the misery of a marriage that is going nowhere. Once again, my friend, Marriage, your time is up.

I had nothing to do with Anthony's marriage failing. God gave man free will to do whatever he chooses. He or she has only to look at himself or herself in the mirror and stare at the person to blame for his or her failure at marriage. Both Nenita and Anthony were to blame. I couldn't care less though. The only thing I wanted and cared about was for one of them to say my name, and for a second time in his life, Anthony, spoke my name into existence. Marriage kept me at bay for a long time during this match, but now the power was in my corner. Anthony had given me the juice I needed to put Marriage on its ass for the ten count. Once my name was spoken, I'd already won. When it comes to marriage, I am like the chapter in The Bible called Revelation. In this day and age, I'm probably only second to Lucifer himself. I'm an immortal thought in Anthony's mind now. I'm the escape he required from all his mistakes in this marriage. Because when my name was spoken, all the mistakes in the marriage come crashing down on the individual like a hammer – all at one time. Anthony is tormented by his failure at marriage for the second time in his life and the memories leave an everlasting impression in his mind for life at his failure again. Even he can't believe some of the things he has done in the destruction of his marriage to Nenita. Anthony had the perfect wife. You couldn't get any more solid than Nenita. Even I knew that. But it still didn't matter. Without that four-letter word resonating in one's heart and mind every minute of the day on your significant other, you will fail Marriage. I will prevail, and you will speak my name. It is inevitable. I am a friend of Anthony, who will always see him through these dark times in his life. My name is DIVORCE. I will ensure Marriage is beaten mercilessly in the ring of life. Not even your god can save you from me. Even with him in your corner, I will plow through Marriage like a buzz saw and have it laid out on the canvas, out for the count. Once the ten count is completed, victory is mine. In this fight however, the one that lays down never gets back up. The psychological trauma of divorce afterwards is of no concern or problem of mine. That's the individual's problem to deal with. Anthony will figure it out just like the last marriage or maybe he won't. I don't care. My name has been spoken. Now, it's time for me to go to work.

As with the first marriage, Anthony got off easy with his marriage to Nenita – if you want to call it that. They had been together for almost ten years. In all those ten years together, they had nothing to show for it but a lot of furniture in which Anthony wanted no part of. No property, no money because Nenita spent it all, and no investments which led to a court hearing in which they were easily divorced with no contesting from both parties. Ten years of wasted time in Anthony and Nenita's life only for both to leave empty handed with nothing but their names. What a waste. This was a bore of a divorce for me just like the first. There was no money, no property, no kids and not much of anything to keep the drama going forward to cause more hate and divide between Anthony and Nenita. In fact, they became friends afterwards as Anthony apologized for not being the best husband he could have been for Nenita. It's always when all is said and done, and there is time to dwell on the past, that one realizes what a failure both parties have been during the marriage. I must give it up to Anthony for apologizing to Nenita for his failure at being a husband. I could only laugh at the possibilities if they had become a team early in the marriage. I saw great potential for their marriage at the beginning. There's always great potential at the beginning for any marriage to succeed. Once the honeymoon is over though, and the realities of real life start to settle in, time will tell where a marriage is headed. And I knew soon after that these two would never become a team. I could zero in on the problem with this marriage, and the bullseye was on Anthony. Whatever his problems are, are of no concern of mine. My work is done here. Altogether, over fourteen years of Anthony's life he has spent married with two women, up to this point. Think about it to yourself – fourteen years of marriage have led to nothing. Those fourteen years have yielded nothing for his financial wellbeing for the future. As you get older, starting over takes a toll on one's finances after divorce. That's your problem to figure out, not mine. All I know is, it's another marriage ended with wealth lost, by yours truly, DIVORCE.

CHAPTER 6

The Challenge

ONCE AGAIN, MY good friend Anthony is single. He is divorced for the second time. I began to weigh on Anthony's conscious. I do that from time to time. I wanted Anthony to realize that I had won, and he was on the losing end again. I weighed in on Anthony's mind so much, he began to see all the failures he committed during his marriage to Janet and Nenita. I wanted him to suffer through all those memories of how he could have prevented the death of both marriages. I wanted him to become enraged at me. I wanted him to want to give marriage another try. I wanted him to want to succeed where I knew he would fail. These thoughts weighed on Anthony's conscious so heavily, he challenged me. He challenged me, DIVORCE. I dare anyone these days to challenge me. My friend Marriage is weak. Without the proper mindset, my friend Marriage is predestined to fail against me. Anthony told me and his god that he would find someone to marry and he would prevail against me this time. Are you speaking to your god or are you speaking to me? He was talking to me out loud like he once used to talk to his god. You wouldn't challenge your god so why do you think you can challenge me? I am DIVORCE. I am more Anthony's god than the one he worships. Anthony told me failure wasn't an option this time around. I laughed at him, the fool. You can tell your god that nonsense but to me, it's music to my ears. Pray and speak to your god all you want to, Anthony! Nothing will ever change what we have between you and me. We were made for each other. You are a walking disaster, and I feed off that. I feed off you. It makes me stronger and pulls me into the forefront of your life. You make Marriage a weakling against me. Marriage doesn't stand a chance against me when it comes to you, Anthony! Anthony again prays to his god to help him find that special someone that he could be with forever. Again, I laughed at him. How pathetic! I accept your challenge, Anthony. How could I not accept? Your track record speaks for itself and the odds are already against you.

My name is DIVORCE. I need my friend Marriage here with me before I can come back into existence. Marriage is a beautiful thing between two people. Even I had to admit that. There's something special when a couple are bonded together with that four-letter word that is powerful enough to keep me at bay. That is to be respected. But when Marriage is in the ring of life against me, DIVORCE, in a match which will decide the fate of existence for each of us, I usually always prevail once my name is spoken. Marriage just doesn't have what it takes to deal with me anymore these days.

So bring it on, Anthony! Your new god awaits your challenge with anticipation.

Anthony had been single now going on for two years. He was living the life as a single man and enjoying it. He bought his first house in South Carolina that unfortunately he could only travel to on the weekends while stationed in Norfolk, Virginia. He had finally reached his dream of home ownership. Anthony saw this home as something to pass down to his children. Life was going well for Anthony. However, he always thought something was missing in his life. He had a stable life now, a large house, but no one to share it with. This is the part I love the most. The human need to have that special someone in their life. It is the draw I relish. Even in the possible face of disaster, a man or a woman will risk it all for the love of a person. They will risk it all whether it is their financial wellbeing, family, or their own sanity. You will see what I mean as you read on. I'm but a distant memory in Anthony's mind now. I lay dormant waiting to see what his next move would be.

Anthony felt the next lady in his life needed to be the one for life. I had taken a toll on his trust of anyone. Anthony wasn't getting any younger. He wanted a family of his own to take care of and watch them grow. This is what everyone wants. This is the need to reproduce and try to create a good life. However, there is a risk involved in wanting such things. I like seeing families having a good time and enjoying life together, but in the end, my name is DIVORCE. I am the destroyer of families. I wonder why I haven't been labeled a god yet. You know, like the god of family destruction; something like that, but you get my point. Anthony needs to succeed in fulfilling his dream of having a family. I myself, will remain dormant in his mind so my name will be furthest from his thoughts. I want him to pursue and fulfill his dream of having a family. Once it is complete, that is when my friends and I go to work.

Anthony struck out at the club with Janet who left him with all the debt during his first marriage. Anthony struck out a second time with Nenita. However, he was the root cause for the end of that marriage. Has Anthony learned anything from his mistakes? I guess we'll find out.

Anthony is trying to think where someone goes to find a nice lady to date. The club is not even on the list of places to find someone to date anymore; maybe for a good one night stand in the sack, but not marriage material. Anthony decides to turn to the new wave of dating – the internet. He goes on to one website, registers, and creates a profile. There, it's done. Anthony then began going through profiles of different women to see if there is anyone he is interested in or is matched with. He did this for almost a month trying to find the perfect woman to possibly date. Then one day, he came across a profile that caught his attention. It was her smile that caught his attention. Out of the hundreds of profiles Anthony had gone through, her smile stuck out to him. He thought to himself this woman was the most beautiful thing he had ever seen. That smile alone caught his attention; now he needed to see what she was all about.

Anthony began reading through her profile to see if they had anything in common. One thing that stood out immediately was that she had one child. Anthony didn't know if he wanted to date a woman with a child. But it seemed that every single women's profile he visited had at least one child. I guess that was one thing he couldn't escape from was being a stepfather. He saw that she was a business administrator, so she had a job. Her interests were somewhat in line with his. He decided to give it a chance and send her a message. With the message sent to this online mystery woman with the pretty smile, now, all Anthony had to do was wait and see if she responded. I like the prospects of this find Anthony has made. I myself was hoping for the best for him. Besides, our challenge to one another can't begin until he finds himself another wife. So, of course, I'm rooting for Anthony. Go get her, Anthony!

A few days later, Anthony checks his email. His online mystery lady from the dating website had sent him a response to his message. The lady's name was Tiana. It was a positive response and he replied. This could be called the feeling-out period between the two. Anthony found out that Tiana was a divorced single parent of one daughter. She worked as a business administrator for a manufacturing company. Anthony and Tiana messaged each other online for over two weeks asking each other questions about their life and what plans each of them had for the future. He liked messaging with Tiana online. Anthony began sending her electronic friendship cards through email to let her know she was on his mind. Tiana liked that a lot. Eventually, the two went from messaging online and decided to make contact with each other by phone. Oh boy! This is looking pretty good so far. They spoke on the phone for several weeks still trying to feel each other out and to see if they were compatible and comfortable talking to one another. When Anthony and Tiana felt comfortable enough with each other over the phone, it was time to meet in person, face to face. They both decided to set up a time to meet at one of Anthony's favorite restaurants. The courtship of this internet lady by Anthony would continue over dinner with one another. This dinner was important for the both of them. I had a good feeling about Tiana. I could tell Anthony was serious about this new prospect. Usually, he would be after the booty but this time, he was actually taking it slow and asked her to dinner. It may be game on sooner rather than later.

I hate boyfriend-girlfriend relationships and the friends with benefits deal. There is no way for me to come into fruition with those types of relationships. I need my friend Marriage to form. The first two marriages that Anthony had were somewhat of a bore when it came to my standards of divorce. There was wealth lost but I want more. I want to show you, the reader, the extent of my true power. You've only seen a small fraction of it but there is more to come. I know it.

I can feel it. I just hope Anthony keeps this one. I will wait until the marriage is a sealed deal between this new couple. Then, I will unleash the full extent of the power I have with all my friends in my corner at Anthony. He is a weak-minded man and he will not be able to resist my strategic moves against him. Lucifer himself smiles upon me. I don't want to be smiled upon by him. I want to be on the same level as Lucifer, if not higher. I am the destroyer of all marriages, not him. You will see why I should be labeled a god soon enough.

Chapter 7

Game On! – Marriage Number 3

ANTHONY AND TIANA started dating regularly. They both had a good time and enjoyed each other's company tremendously. They grew closer as the months went on. However, a curve ball was thrown at their budding relationship when it was getting off to such a good start. The ship Anthony was stationed on was conducting a homeport shift to the west coast. This really sucked! Things were going so well. When the ship left the east coast and made its way to the west coast, Anthony kept in contact with Tiana via email. Once the ship arrived in its new homeport on the west coast, Anthony was already in his window to transfer back over to the east coast. He requested to be stationed near a shore duty facility near Tiana. His request was granted and four months later, he was back in his home on the east coast.

    Tiana's house was four hours away from Anthony's house. He drove to Tiana's house and stayed with her until he had to report to his duty station. Living together helped both of them see each other's personalities up close and personal. I stayed hidden deep inside

Anthony's thoughts, so he wouldn't even have a chance to think about me. I wanted him to have a clear mind to seal the deal. I needed him to marry Tiana. For a couple that just decided to live together, they were quite successful at it. Anthony did a good job with Tiana's daughter. They were a small functioning family. I liked that a lot.

Then one day, Tiana spoke two words to Anthony that were music to my ears.

Tiana said, "I'm pregnant."

This news was outstanding! Anthony played the game of house with Tiana, and he found himself with a pregnant girlfriend. When Tiana said that, I could see the thoughts racing through Anthony's head. But, they were happy thoughts. Not thoughts like, 'I made a mistake,' or 'now I'm stuck.' Anthony was happy to finally become a father. In his mind, he had found the perfect lady in Tiana to have a child with. Anthony wanted to marry Tiana before the child was born. He didn't want a child born out of wedlock. There was only one major problem with Anthony marrying Tiana though – HE WAS NOT IN LOVE WITH HER. There goes that four-letter word again. Even though I hate that four-letter word with a passion, it's very powerful. That is why it must be respected. I do respect the power of that four-letter word. It is the only thing that can hold me at bay. It drains me to say that four-letter word. One thing I must admit about God; he had a great system of checks and balances in place to keep everything in check. Love is what gives my friend

Marriage its power to defeat me in the ring of life. Without it, Marriage doesn't have a chance against me and the friends in my corner. Just saying it drains me of power I need to overpower Marriage. I must be careful when it comes to Love. However, since Anthony is not in love with Tiana, this will be an easy victory. I knew Anthony wasn't in love with Tiana. Anthony felt he could eventually fall in love with Tiana as his wife as time went on. This was a big chance Anthony was taking that he would fall in love with Tiana. He hoped this gamble would pay off in the future. I myself thought this was a brilliant plan on Anthony's part. Marrying someone you don't even love? With Anthony's track record for marriage, marrying Tiana without even loving her was everything I could have ever asked for. I hid even deeper in Anthony's thoughts so he wouldn't even think of my name. I wanted this marriage to happen. I will show Anthony that he should never challenge me. Not even his god can help him withstand my assault on his marriage to Tiana. I will unleash every friend I have on him and his new wife – once the nuptials have been said and sealed with a kiss. Ah yes, the wedding. That first kiss from your bride or groom can lead to a lifetime of happiness or seal your fate to a miserable existence with you possibly coming out the back end in a pile of shit. Game on, Anthony! Game on!

Anthony proposed to Tiana by surprise singing a sweet ballad and asking her to marry him. Tiana had tears in her eyes as Anthony sang to her and pulled out the engagement ring. This was so romantic. I love this oh so much. Reading Anthony's mind, he had to get up the courage to sing this song to her. The song sang of how much Tiana meant to him, and he thinks of her with every beat of his heart. But Anthony did it for show. A song like this should flow from the heart. Without true love in his heart, it was a chore to sing for Anthony. Love should make everything easy to do if you love someone with all your heart. He didn't love Tiana at all. Anthony liked Tiana very much but that like hadn't turned into love yet. Anthony wanted to love Tiana so badly, but they hadn't been together long enough to bond into a loving couple. The sex between Anthony and Tiana was awesome. However, in the business of marriage, sex is only one part of the many facets that hold a couple together. If sex was the only thing this marriage had going for it for the foreseeable future, then my chances of winning this challenge against Anthony and his god have risen substantially. You will learn why that four-letter word is so important when entering into a contract such as marriage. Marriage is a contract, and my job is to break that contract between a married couple that have failed to meet the requirements of a happy existence together under their god.

So, I will watch as Anthony makes plans to get married for the third time. You would think Anthony would have given up on the institution as the statistics are against him for a successful third try. But Anthony doesn't know anything about the statistics. All he knows is that he wants to marry this lady whom he doesn't even love. I like his optimism as he thinks that he will be married to Tiana forever. She apparently is everything he ever wanted in a wife. Pretty, smart, great mother, good in bed, and had her own life prior to him coming into the picture. But, once they are married and combine what they both have together, it can only add to the success for both of them in the future. I'm rooting for you, Anthony.

Anthony and Tiana were married by the Justice of the Peace. The deal was signed, sealed, and delivered. They are now pronounced man and wife from here until the end of time. At least that's what most couples think. Your chances of meeting up with me are greater than dying with the one you claimed you loved when you got married under the laws of matrimony. Anthony and Tiana along with Tiana's daughter, Gayle, created the perfect small family. I love seeing small families starting out. It's such a beautiful thing.

Tiana went to work while Anthony stayed home on leave until he had to report to his ultimate duty station. He got bored just sitting around the townhouse, so he decided to go on the internet. I love the internet. It's one of my new friends in this digital age of marriage. While on the internet, Anthony saw a female friend of his from the navy online. This friend saw him online and sent out a chat request to him which Anthony accepted. Awesome! This is the beginning of the end of any trust that was established between Tiana and Anthony. Anthony never thought he was weak, but I knew that he was. Curiosity is one of his most fatal flaws because his curiosity always leads to my best friend in the whole world – INFIDELITY. Even though Anthony never physically met or touched his internet chat friend, Tiana didn't know about this friend which made it a secret. I like secrets between couples. It makes what comes next when the other spouse finds out about the secret worth the wait. Trust is solid at the beginning, but when trust is lost in a marriage, there is no hope of a recovery. This always plays into my favor. In Anthony's mind, he hadn't done anything wrong, so no harm was done. That's until Tiana comes home and looks through the computer's history and sees this little chat session he had going on with his female friend. An argument ensues between Anthony and Tiana, and that, my friend, was the beginning of the decline in trust Tiana had for Anthony in this fledgling marriage. That's one point for me, Anthony, and zero for you.

While pregnant, Tiana was very conscious about her weight and appearance. Weight and Appearance, especially with females, are very important in keeping their self-esteem high about themselves. During Tiana's pregnancy, she was very mindful about how she was gaining weight. Anthony would praise Tiana about her weight saying he liked the way she carried the weight and she was beautiful to him. Then on another occasion, he would say something without thinking. Tiana liked sleeping with her leg on Anthony. One night, with Tiana's leg on him, Anthony turned over and said, 'Get your heavy leg off me.' Wow! Talk about an insensitive person to the needs of his pregnant wife whose hormones were in overdrive, making her sensitive to everything that was said about her. Tiana turned over upset and angry at what Anthony had said while he blissfully went right back to sleep. Anthony would do this a few more times during Tiana's pregnancy without thinking about his wife's feelings. That's two points for me, Anthony, and zero for you for your insensitivity.

After Anthony's previous two marriages to women who ruined his finances, he kept watch over the joint bank account he and Tiana owned like a hawk. He kept a watch over the finances so much that Tiana was hesitant to make a big purchase or anything without consulting Anthony first. However, Tiana saw Anthony make purchases without her consent all the time. Tiana felt Anthony controlled her like a child when it came to the finances. Anthony managed the finances with an iron fist and ensured there was no money used without a consultation with him first. This caused Tiana to resent the way Anthony kept such a tight grip on the finances. Her mind raced whenever she was out shopping whether she could buy something or not which became frustrating for her. Anthony confronted her about a purchase that brought Tiana to tears because of the way he spoke to her. My friend Finances has put Anthony's fear of going broke and in debt again in overdrive to the point he has his wife living in fear of making a purchase. You may think you are not going to carry any baggage from your previous marriage into the next but guess again. This baggage from your previous marriage always reappears without you even thinking or knowing about it. Anthony thinks everything is fine but it isn't. That's three points for me, Anthony, and zero for you because of your Gestapo-like attitude toward the finances.

Tiana gave birth to a beautiful baby girl they named Jade. It was a hard birth for Tiana. Anthony wanted another child. Like any man, Anthony wanted a son. He was banking on this next child to be a son. However, Tiana said she was done having children. Anthony convinced her to have one more. Tiana decided to have one more child for Anthony and that was it. This time, she bore a son who they called Jevon. Anthony was a great father to his children. However, it seemed he forgot about Gayle, his stepdaughter. Tiana reminded him that Gayle was his daughter as well. This right here is the beginning of the end of a good relationship between a stepfather and stepdaughter. Tiana has been carefully watching this and if Anthony can't be a father to her daughter, there will be problems in the future. I've seen this dozens of times before. The man gets so involved with his own offspring, he forgets about the child that was there first and alienates the stepchild. That child resents that parent that now doesn't show them any attention like before and becomes jealous of the stepfather's children. The mother begins to resent the stepfather for not being a father to her child. Anthony has created a recipe for disaster and he still thinks everything is fine. He is oblivious to the fact that his relationship with his wife and stepdaughter are tarnished. This is what I like. Anthony might as well be on my side. This recipe he has created is simmering right now. I can't wait until it starts boiling over. That's four points for me, Anthony, and zero for you.

One day, when the couple were in bed, Tiana was talking to Anthony. Anthony was listening to her speak and thinking about what he had gotten himself into. The thoughts hit him like a ton of bricks. He couldn't believe he was thinking these thoughts, but he was. Anthony didn't like Tiana. In fact, Tiana annoyed Anthony. He compared Tiana to Nenita, his second wife. At least he liked being around Nenita. He disliked being around Tiana. He thought that by this time, he would have fallen madly in love with her, but it didn't happen. I myself was enjoying these thoughts going on in Anthony's mind. This was outstanding. A husband that doesn't love or even like his wife. Now, Anthony realizes what a big mistake he had made by marrying Tiana. It was then and there he thought he should have just paid child support rather than marry this woman he didn't even like. To Anthony, Tiana was goofy and annoying. He understood why her sisters treated her differently now. Tiana even told Anthony on multiple occasions that she felt he didn't like her. When the lady you've married feels like she isn't liked by her husband, there's a problem. Anthony kept telling Tiana she was crazy and he loved her. I just laughed every time he said that. What a liar Anthony has turned out to be. This isn't anything new to me though. He didn't have any love for Tiana at all. All Anthony and Tiana had was sex between them, nothing more. They rarely did anything together. Their interests were totally separate from one another. Anthony wasn't a people person but Tiana was. They didn't even go out shopping together. This married couple was living separate lives while married. Marriages like these are made in my version of heaven. Anthony can't even hide his displeasure of being married to Tiana anymore. It's easy to spot when that four-letter word is not involved in a marriage. I'm up by five points, Anthony. You will have to give your life to the Lord your God again to make this marriage a success. I don't see that happening though as we continue on a downward slope towards disaster.

Anthony's time was up on shore duty and it was time for him to transfer back to sea duty in Norfolk, Virginia. He asked Tiana to move with him to his duty station but she refused. Anthony knew right then and there that Tiana's refusal to move the family with him to Norfolk was the final nail in the coffin for their marriage. Without the stability of his wife and family to back him and keep him grounded, Norfolk would eventually consume Anthony as it did with his previous marriages. He was a broken man without Tiana by his side. Anthony was not strong enough to withstand the lure of debauchery that Norfolk offered a married man which was a lot to handle. Anthony transferred to Norfolk to a ship manned by men and women. This didn't sit well with Tiana because she didn't want Anthony working around any women – which was impossible. Anthony wasn't even allowed to make friends with any of the women he worked with. There were no such things as female friends in the navy when it came to Anthony according to Tiana. Communication between Anthony and Tiana dwindled during this separation. The only time Anthony went home was during the weekends when he didn't have duty. This was the strain on this marriage that I was looking for. I must hand it to Tiana. She gave it her best try at trying to keep this marriage going while Anthony alienated her and did as he pleased.

On one of Anthony's many trips home, Tiana decided to go through Anthony's car and she found a surprising item inside which she revealed to Anthony – a used condom. One thing Anthony developed into was a horrible liar. He lied so much he couldn't even keep up with his lies anymore. Tiana couldn't tell if Anthony was telling the truth or not anymore. Anthony had lied so much that when Tiana made a conclusion about the lie, it usually was the wrong one, but she stuck with it and believed it. Ah, that word Trust is the solid foundation in which a marriage thrives. Without it, you might as well make plans to say my name. Tiana, as usual, got upset about the condom, made Anthony sleep on the couch for a few days, but then she forgave him. Tiana was such a forgiving person. I admired her. This pot that continues to boil has the cover on, but it was about to overflow and create a fire in the kitchen. Anthony knew he would never gain the trust of Tiana again after that stunt. Anthony figured since his time in the navy was almost up, when he retired, things should be different. What Anthony didn't realize was things can't be different if you don't love your wife. All I have to do is sit back and watch as this marriage spirals out of control. I don't even keep score anymore. One way or another, Anthony or Tiana will say my name. Count on it!

CHAPTER 8

Revelations of Impending Doom

ANTHONY RETIRED FROM the Navy after nearly twenty-four years. He moved his family to his hometown of Savannah, Georgia to operate a convenience store he had bought. Even though Anthony and Tiana's marriage was not the greatest, they had a convenience store, two houses that they rented, and had saved a considerable amount of money through investments in stocks. They had acquired assets for future wealth building and were on track to acquire more.

One of the many things I loved about Anthony was that his priorities were all screwed up. He didn't support Tiana on anything. Tiana told Anthony that she might be up for a leadership role at the company she was working for. Anthony told her she didn't have what it takes to be in charge at her company. This was not being a supportive husband at all. Instead of congratulating his wife, he knocked her down. Tiana went in for surgery to have her tummy tucked and have breast implants. Anthony thought it was a waste of money and he didn't even support Tiana on her decision to have surgery. He didn't even go to the hospital or bring her back – he worked. Tiana resented Anthony for not supporting her on anything in her life. Tiana even had issues with renting her home, and Anthony did nothing to help her. Not helping her forced Tiana to eventually sell the home. She barely broke even. Anthony had realized the potential in the townhouse but did nothing to help Tiana save the house. If he had stepped in, the house could have been salvaged and used as a rental property for the benefit of the family's future. He chose not to and allowed wealth to slip through his fingers.

 Anthony and Tiana lived together as man and wife but began to live totally separate lives from one another. Anthony did his thing, and Tiana did hers. They did absolutely nothing together. The only time they came together was when they had sex. The love Tiana had for Anthony at the beginning began to turn to dislike. Anthony was an asshole. Even he knew that. His relationship with his stepdaughter, Gayle, had deteriorated to the point they rarely spoke. Anthony realized the time away from his family while in Norfolk was damaging. He decided to make a concerted effort to try and salvage his marriage along with his family. Anthony and Tiana even went to church to ask their god to help them with their marriage. They even said vows to each other saying this was a new start in their marriage. Again, I laughed. Without that four-letter word in Anthony's heart, this marriage was on its way to a dead end. The only person who will be at that dead end waiting will be me because one of them will see me and say my name. Still, I promise you.

    No matter how many times Anthony tried to make his marriage work, he ended up returning to what he was used to doing – which was being an uncaring and unsupportive husband to Tiana. Anthony began thinking about his marriage. They were going on almost ten years of marriage together. Their marriage wasn't growing anymore. They were not a team and never were. He thought back to the day when he thought to himself about not loving Tiana but marrying her anyway because she was carrying his child. That was when he realized he had made the biggest mistake of his life in marrying Tiana. He should have just paid the child support. Now, he was stuck in a marriage that was going nowhere. Tiana and him rarely spoke to each other anymore. They kept out of each other's way. In a last-ditch effort to save their marriage, Anthony and Tiana went to marriage counseling. Counseling turned out to be a disaster. The only thing that it did was bring up bad memories for the pair, so they stopped going. Tiana was on Anthony's mind most days. He asked himself the question, what if Tiana died today, would he cry at her funeral? Anthony didn't have to take a long time to answer that question. The answer was no, he wouldn't cry for Tiana if she died. That was a revelation that Anthony didn't want to accept, but he had no choice. He had no love whatsoever for Tiana. He proved it to his own self by placing himself in the situation of Tiana dying. The thought of Tiana's death didn't do anything to Anthony – no tears or anything came upon him. That was when Anthony realized he had no love for the mother of his children. Anthony also came to the conclusion that was why all his marriages had failed miserably. He didn't really love any of the women he had married. The truth finally surfaces for Anthony to see why he has failed at marriage three times. And as the saying goes, the truth shall set you free. I am waiting to set you free Anthony.

Tiana wanted to get rid of Anthony. She wanted to get him out of the house. My counterpart in her mind was working overtime as well. She began plotting and planning on a way to get Anthony removed from the house. This was not dislike anymore. This was pure hatred working in the mind of Tiana. She began pestering and making life miserable for Anthony every day he came home in hopes he would leave or better yet, strike her. Anthony had a feeling Tiana had something planned but he wasn't sure. All he concentrated on was being a good father to his children. Tiana finally thought of a brilliant way to get rid of Anthony. This marriage was eventually going to end, but it was headed for a finish that even I could have never imagined. Tiana had only hate swirling around in her mind for Anthony. This was a toxic environment to live in and Anthony knew it. One way or another something was going to happen. Whatever it was, I waited in anticipation for it to happen.

One of the many arguments Anthony and Tiana always had was about him turning off the alarm clock and not waking Tiana up. Well, Anthony did it again one morning, and Tiana saw an opportunity to get him. She argued with Anthony about shutting off the alarm clock. She tried to get a rise out of Anthony but he kept laughing at her ridiculous argument which pissed her off even more. It pissed Tiana off so much she viciously struck Anthony on the side of his head. This had now become a physical confrontation initiated by Tiana. Tiana had just committed domestic violence against her husband, Anthony. I wasn't even counting on this but this situation kept getting better and better. Anthony took the shot Tiana gave him. He shrugged it off. Anthony then playfully tried to tap Tiana's bun on top of her head to show her that she didn't faze him. Unfortunately, the tap went bad and he missed his mark grazing Tiana's nose with his finger causing a nosebleed. Anthony was stunned. I couldn't be happier for what Anthony did to Tiana. He just poured more gasoline onto an already combustible situation. Tiana dialed 911 and called the police on Anthony. She told the 911 operator that Anthony assaulted her and she was bleeding from the nose. Anthony stood and listened as his wife, Tiana, told the 911 operator what happened – except the part where she had struck Anthony. Anthony was in shock. He waited for the arrival of the police outside to take him away. This would be the last time these two would see each other as man and wife. It took pure hatred to do what Tiana did to Anthony. It was what she was waiting on; an opening to get rid of Anthony. This marriage was finally over. But, I'm waiting on my name to be spoken to bring me back to life. Then, and only then, will this marriage be headed down the road Anthony has failed for the third time in his life – the road to me, DIVORCE. I couldn't help but laugh as I saw Anthony's life crumble before his very eyes. The woman Anthony has been married to for close to ten years lied and framed him with domestic violence to remove him from the house. I've been around for ions and this has been one of my most notable marriages that has crashed and burned. I love it. The first two marriages ended in boredom but this marriage ended with a bang – just how I like it.

Chapter 9

I Always Win in the End

WEALTH. WHAT IS wealth when it comes to marriage? Do you think its money? That's only a small part of what's lost when a marriage ends. When it comes to marriage, wealth can be broken down into many things. When two people seek me for divorce, all love is gone. Hearts are broken, future dreams are shattered, and lives are changed forever. The only thing left tangible to salvage from a broken marriage is money. And believe me when I say, money is what it's all about. It's all about self-preservation now in the mind of Tiana. There was no love in this marriage. There was a mutual respect between Anthony and Tiana at one time, but there is only hate that remains between them now. This marriage once had great possibilities for the future. If they had stayed together, life would have been a whole lot simpler for the both of them. But now, it's complicated. Disdain for one another will be the relationship between them from now and forever into the future. In terms of money, with Anthony's military retirement, Tiana knew she would be getting a percentage of that plus any monetary assets that he owned. Most of all,

Tiana knew, she would be taking Anthony's favorite prize from him – his retirement home. It was Tiana who initiated and said my name first when she met with one of my favorite supporters – an attorney.

Tiana said to her attorney, "I want a divorce due to domestic violence against me."

I love lies. Lies revolve around me like planets. Lies are what makes a divorce go around. My name is DIVORCE. A divorce is not right unless there are lies involved. The lies started to mount from the very moment my name was spoken and I was born again. I could feel the hatred within Tiana. The anger for a marriage she put so much work into, and now, it was over. Anthony did the same thing when he met with his attorney which strengthened me. He met Tiana's lies with lies of his own. DIVORCE was born again and it was time for me to go to work.

Through the attorneys, mediators, and then the judge, who couldn't care less about Anthony, Tiana, or their children, the family house was to be sold and the proceeds separated between Anthony and Tiana. This was one of my favorites because it pissed Anthony off – because that house was meant for his children when he passed on. If he didn't have anything else to leave them, he would have the house they grew up in paid off and an asset for them. His pure hatred for Tiana led him to sell the house. In Anthony's mind, if he couldn't have his house, his enemy sure was not going to enjoy what he had worked for all his life. Oh well, I guess Anthony must purchase another house to pass on to his children.

Tiana could care less about the house. Her only motive in life was to hurt Anthony. Tiana didn't even put a dime into the house Anthony bought, and she gets half the proceeds. I could feel the rage in Anthony as he sat back and wished all types of things he could do to kill Tiana in that instant. This is where divorce gets dangerous. Thoughts like what Anthony had going through his mind could lead to realms that I have seen before. Thoughts like these have brought down many a good men and women who ended up having to do time in prison due to the hatred of their spouse. The emotion of anger is most dangerous of all during divorce. Feelings and emotions are centered on hurting the other partner as much as possible for the years wasted in a marriage that seemed promising at the beginning. Anthony contains his anger for Tiana but the thoughts are there no matter what he tries to do. Another case of wealth that was lost through divorce. Tiana, of course, being the woman would be granted custody of the children along with child support and spousal support for several years. In his affidavit against Tiana, Anthony wrote concern for the children's' well being in the care of Tiana. Unfortunately during divorce, the judge could care less about what's written. They don't even read the affidavits. So, Anthony's concerns are overlooked. That's the courts for you. Just like an assembly line, it's the judge's job to quickly end the marriage and move on to the next case on his itinerary. The judge could care less for what was on the affidavit or for the children. And as for spousal and child support, for a woman who was a successful administrator who could earn just as much as Anthony, Tiana still wanted alimony which was music to my ears. This is the, 'I'm going to hurt you where it hurts the most' attitude. I love it. So, Anthony can't advance far in life until his alimony and child support are finished. The judge even gave Tiana an order to get back to full-time work which she failed to do. It was overlooked by the judge when she passed up that she was unemployed because it was a different judge this time and he didn't even blink an eye at it. He overlooked what the previous judge said and let it slide without even a reprimand. You have to love the courts. The family court is totally fucked up and I love it! Tiana's underhanded moves were music to my ears. Now we move on to my biggest supporters in these cases – the attorneys. When there are attorneys there are attorneys' fees. Anthony wanted to go to court over the alimony, but his attorney said if he went to court, he would more than likely have to pay his wife's attorney's fees. Like I said before, DIVORCE IS HELL, just like war. And believe me when I say this was war. Either way, everyone loses in the end. There are no winners when it comes to me. Only I win. My hand will be raised in victory as I watch Marriage slowly wither away after the ten count in the ring of life. My friend Marriage is once again no more. I reign supreme once again. You have personally seen my power. I have broken a bond that the man up high created. Not even Lucifer can do that – only me.

If the kids must suffer under a mother that has no

scruples and lied to the police to get rid of her husband, the judge does not care. He didn't even read the affidavits. Divorce court is meant to shuffle ending marriages out the door as fast as possible to move on to the next case. The attorneys and courts threaten the two individuals with having to pay their spouses attorneys' fees if they have an objection to the mediation. Anthony wanted to prove that Tiana lied about the domestic violence charge and she was not fit to raise their children. Due to the divorce being a no-fault divorce, those allegations are a wash now. Tiana's lies are what helped her. This is a woman after my own heart. My associates ensure nothing but the best for each client when it comes to your representation. Anthony and Tiana poured thousands of dollars into the pockets of these lawyers, mediators, and the court system. That's what the court system is all about – draining you dry of all your money. And you have to think, what if Anthony had gotten arrested the day Tiana called the police and lied about the domestic violence against her? He would have been sent to jail, he could have possibly lost his job and would have lost his steady stream of income that paid his bills. Tiana was so filled with hate and rage, she didn't know she was hurting her own self and the kids by doing this to Anthony. I love blind rage. Especially when it comes to a vindictive bitch such as Tiana. She is a woman after my own heart. This is a divorce for the ages. This is what I wanted to show you the world and Anthony what true hate in divorce is like and what the outcome is. Talk about a vicious bitch who wanted to see the demise of her soon to be ex-husband. That's pure hate. That's what I want to see in a divorce – pure hatred for one another at the end. I love Tiana. Hate is the greatest recipe for divorce because it lacks any feeling or sense of humanity towards the person they once loved. Just think about it for a second. At one time, these two people were inseparable and now they hate each other more than life itself right now. Think of all the things they could have done for their kids with close to thirty thousand dollars in legal fees by the time it was all over. Those kids won't see any piece of that money. That's money going towards my cause. I am DIVORCE. I live a lavish lifestyle and it takes money to satisfy me. You can think of me as a gold digger.

Money, money, money is all that we talk about. You will find that divorce is more than money. It encompasses everything involved in destroying a family. A cohesive family is strong and successful. That four letter word is very powerful in a strong family unit. It takes massive amounts of power to break that four letter word and crumble the very foundations of a family. Let's talk about the other wealth that's called family. Anthony and Tiana's kids are having trouble adjusting without Daddy always being there as it was Daddy who was their guiding light and strong rock that never let them down. Now, he's gone. The kids are having issues concentrating at school because their mother and father are getting divorced. Tiana has to lie to her kids and say that Daddy initiated the violence against her. Can you believe this woman? Her treachery has and shows no bounds. Anthony actually tells the truth to his kids. However, they don't know who is telling the truth and are confused because they love both of their parents. This unfortunately hinders the children in school and in life. Both will require therapy and hopefully get on the right track back to a normal life. Life is already abnormal for them without the constant presence of a father in the house. They say war is hell. DIVORCE is hell.

Without a father present in the house, who will the daughter latch on to when she needs a man in her life to figure complicated life situations that only a man would know? How will the son break out of his shell of being someone that stays in the house all day and doesn't know how to lose or win at life? The kids used to go to piano lessons, but Tiana has too many things going on in her life now to take them and support the development of her kids in the arts. The daughter played the violin and the son played the piano. All that hard work and effort are a thing of the past without the father in the house motivating and guiding them. Anthony has visions of his son growing effeminate in his absence in a house of females. It almost drives him crazy to think about it. The father worked at night to be there for his kids during the day. They would ride their bikes everyday they had the chance. Tiana is to consumed with herself to take the time to ride bikes with the children. As you can see, it was Anthony who took care of the kids, not Tiana. The courts totally overlooked that. That's how blind the courts are when it comes to divorce. The courts think they know everything when they actually don't know anything. My name is DIVORCE. What happens to your kids is of no concern of mine. My job is to end marriages and families. I don't provide anything afterwards but misery and memories of what could have been.

DIVORCE is hell on kids. But that is of no concern of mine. They are nothing but casualties in my never-ending war with Marriage. If you have a problem with me, maybe you should concentrate and talk with Marriage first. Instead of speaking with me first, you should speak with Marriage first. Maybe you wouldn't be in this situation if you had spoken with my best friend Marriage first. Because once you say my name, I will be first in your life until the end.

Anthony is forced to get his own place far from the nice neighborhood he was used to and still provide for his family. Well, I should say, his son, daughter, and ex-wife. So now he has two households he has to provide for – which can be quite expensive. Anthony thinks back to when he made the decision to marry someone he didn't love. It was the biggest mistake he ever made, and it cost him almost everything he had worked for all those years to acquire. Anthony can't even fully retire now due to everything he has to pay out to a wife he didn't love who falsely accused him of domestic violence. It's eating him up inside. It torments him daily. Adding up all the time lost due to his third marriage failing adds up to nearly twenty-five years of wealth and time lost that Anthony will never get back in his life again. It's almost like money you lost out on in the stock market and then having to sell the stock. That money is gone forever – just like future wealth for Anthony and his kids. The only thing keeping him together is his love for his children. There goes that four-letter word again. Many a man has fallen because of the reality of my win over them. I must admit though, Anthony was using that love for his kids to hold himself together. He will pursue his former wife for custody and dump more money into the hands of a lawyer not because he hates Tiana and trust me, he hates her with a passion, but because he loves his kids and wants to raise them in his image. So this saga doesn't end, it continues here on after.

My name is DIVORCE. I claim victory over you, Anthony. You lose. When you lose against me, you lose everything. You lose big. Remember, wealth isn't just about money. It's family, time, happiness, and peace of mind that encompasses the wealth of an individual and the people around them. Those are all gone because of me. That's my job. There are always the what ifs, but it's too late for what ifs, Anthony and Tiana. It's over. It's time to move on. I watch as Anthony looks at other married couples and wishes he had the same magic they have in their marriage. Now Anthony will more than likely never marry again. Anthony and Tiana are damaged goods for anyone seeking to form a relationship with them. That's what happens when you say my name. I will damage and scar you for life. You will never be the same again. That, of course, is of no concern of mine. I leave that in your hands to figure out and try to overcome. The aftermath of my destruction in Anthony and Tiana's life will live on for years to come not only in their minds, but in the minds of their children as well.

I should be a god by now. I don't need the man up high or that guy sitting at his right hand to know that my power is stronger than anything he could throw at me. He was not my god. He can take that four-letter word and shove it up his ass for all I care. It means nothing to me like it did with Anthony and Tiana. My destructive path through marriage is unequaled. You get married under your god and then you are divorced by your new god – me! Because of this failure in your marriage, I have become my own being. Screw Lucifer, this is my realm to play, and I do as I please. When you come before me, you will say my name. Your God has given you one of the greatest gifts in life – free will. Free will to make decisions that are good and those that could be detrimental for your future. You can never be angry at me because each person has the free will to make their own decisions in life. I'm just the middleman who helps you break the bond you've created under your god. So, to all you single men, women, and couples out there who want to get married, I encourage the institution of marriage wholeheartedly so don't be afraid of me. I'm not your enemy. You can use me as a tool or anything that you need when the time comes. Because, the odds are already against you when you bond with my best friend Marriage. I'm your friend until the very end. Because when the love is all dried up and gone, the sweet memories of yesterday have passed, and you want to be released from your contract of marriage – all you have to do is say my name. I can't promise you'll be happy with the results I provide you, but I will release you just as I have done for millions of other people. Only through me can the bond that was created under your god be broken. It takes lots of power, strength, and help to break this bond. That four-letter word can't save you. Do not ever blame me for what you have brought upon yourself. You have only to look in the mirror and know who to point the finger at for all that has happened and befallen you. My friend Marriage is on the ropes in the ring of life and about to take my knockout punch once you say my name. Only I can do that and I will do it with sincerity because you and I are in this together. I want you to always keep in mind that in the end – I always win. Winning for you however, may not be as sweet as you think. Don't ever think this will be a happy ending because it won't. It never is. When it's all said and done, you will be kneeling at my feet begging for mercy. You will always lose more than you know. Now, Anthony is at his second job trying to make ends meet until he can pull himself out of this financial rut he has placed himself in. I listen to his thoughts. He's angry at how his life has turned out for him. He should be enjoying life after retiring from the Navy, but instead he's hating life. All the bad decisions he's made in the past when it came to marriage finally began to sink in. This final marriage has devastated his life. He doesn't even want to be seen in public anymore until his life is back on track. Tiana is no different. I listen to her thoughts. After giving so much to this marriage and to have it self-destruct in her face has turned her bitter and angry at Anthony and the world. Tiana thinks that her lying to the police to get Anthony out of the house was justified. Her thinking had become warped. She cannot even think clearly anymore after this ordeal. She's a walking time bomb and volatile. Anthony and Tiana continue to trade barbs over instant messaging on their phones constantly trying to one up the other in a financial war of assets between the two. The battle and war of hate with these two will continue until the day each one of them enters the grave. The loving bond between these two has been broken by yours truly and replaced with a deep hatred for one another that will never be resolved or forgiven. I just stand in the middle and watch as these two wastes their lives hating each other while their kids are caught in the crossfire of this war of nasty words and feelings towards one another that the kids can pick up on immediately. How sad. Don't look at me like that. I just broke the bond that God and Marriage had between Anthony and Tiana. The rest is mans' free will to do as he pleases after the bond is broken. I just sit back and watch the chaos in the aftermath. My work is done here. It's time for me to move on to my next subject. I don't like to use the term victim. It sounds like I'm some kind of predator seeking to intentionally end marriages when in fact it goes back to one of God's greatest gifts to man – FREE WILL. Free will to make the choice to end a marriage if that person wishes it. That's my job. That has always been my calling. I'm an innocent bystander in all of this. At the very end of your marriage, I am your new god now. I control your mind, your thoughts, your actions. Both Anthony and Tiana belong to me now. When Anthony and Tiana eventually sit down and think deeply about what they have done to one another, they will finally realize, all it is and all that it will ever be in the end, is wealth lost, by yours truly, DIVORCE.